Such a Fuss

Written by Roderick Hunt

Illustrated by Nick Schon,
based on the original characters
created by Alex Brychta

OXFORD
UNIVERSITY PRESS

Read these words

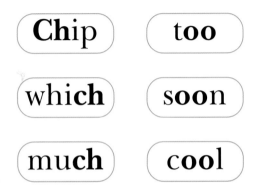

Chip   too

which   soon

much   cool

Dad had six hens.

Chip had a hen, too.

"This is Viv," said Chip.

Biff got the eggs.

She put them in a box.

The hens ran up.
Chip fed them.

11

"Viv is upset," said Chip.

"Such a fuss," said Biff.

13

Chip put the hens to bed.

But Viv did not go in.

Biff and Chip hid in the shed.

A fox got in.

The fox ran off.

"I can soon fix the pen,"
said Dad.

"Viv is a cool hen," said Chip.

Talk about the story

Who has
six hens?

What is
Chip's hen called?

Why was
Viv upset?

What kind
of pet would you
like to have?

21

Missing letters

Choose an ending for the words.

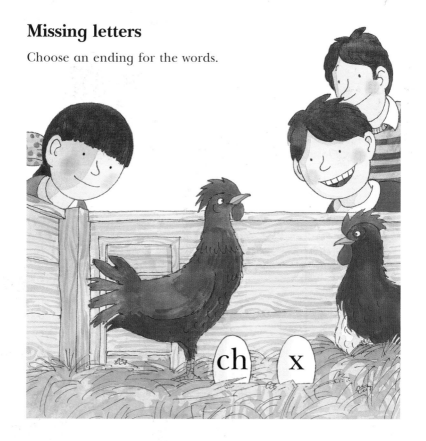

ri _____   fo _____   mu _____

si _____   su _____   bo _____